Sniff!

Written by
Sue Graves

Illustrated by
Lisa Smith

FRANKLIN WATTS
LONDON • SYDNEY

Sue Graves
"Having a cold isn't much fun, is it? I bet Sniff felt much happier when he found his squeaky toy!"

Lisa Smith
"I have been drawing ever since I was small. I don't have a dog, but if I did I would like one just like Sniff to help me find things!"

Sniff the dog was good at sniffing.

He found Dad's sock.

7

He found Mum's keys.

He found Ellie's lunch!

11

One day, Sniff got a cold.
He couldn't sniff.

Sniff couldn't find
his squeaky toy.

"Poor Sniff," said Ellie.
"Let's help him find it."

Everyone looked ...
but they couldn't find it.

Sniff was sad.
He went to bed.

21

"Sniff can't sniff!" laughed Ellie, "but he found his squeaky toy!"

Notes for parents and teachers

READING CORNER has been structured to provide maximum support for new readers. The stories may be used by adults for sharing with young children. Primarily, however, the stories are designed for newly independent readers, whether they are reading these books in bed at night, or in the reading corner at school or in the library.

Starting to read alone can be a daunting prospect. **READING CORNER** helps by providing visual support and repeating words and phrases, while making reading enjoyable. These books will develop confidence in the new reader, and encourage a love of reading that will last a lifetime!

If you are reading this book with a child, here are a few tips:

1. Talk about the story before you start reading. Look at the cover and the title. What might the story be about? Why might the child like it?

2. Encourage the child to reread the story, and to retell the story in their own words, using the illustrations to remind them what has happened.

3. Discuss the story and see if the child can relate it to their own experience, or perhaps compare it to another story they know.

4. Give praise! Small mistakes need not always be corrected.

READING CORNER covers three grades of early reading ability, with three levels at each grade. Each level has a certain number of words per story, indicated by the number of bars on the spine of the book, to allow you to choose the right book for a young reader:

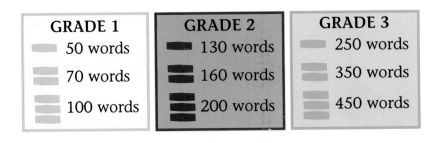

GRADE 1	GRADE 2	GRADE 3
50 words	130 words	250 words
70 words	160 words	350 words
100 words	200 words	450 words